Year Zero

by Michael Golamco

SAMUEL FRENCH

FOUNDED 1830

NEW YORK HOLLYWOOD LONDON TORONTO

SAMUELFRENCH.COM

ISBN 978-0-573-69939-9   Printed in U.S.A.   #29756

MUSIC USE NOTE

IMPORTANT BILLING AND CREDIT REQUIREMENTS

YEAR ZERO was first produced by Victory Gardens (Dennis Zacek, Artistic Director; Jan Kallish, Executive Director) in Chicago, Illinois in September 2009 as part of their Ignition Festival of new plays (Sandy Shinner, Producer of Ignition). The performance was directed by Andrea J. Dymond, with sets by Richard and Jacqueline Penrod, costumes by Frances Maggio, lighting by Mary Badger, sound by Kyle Irwin, props by Grant Sabin, and fight choreography by David Woolley. The production stage manager was Rachel Robinson. The cast was as follows:

GLENN . . . . .Allan Aquino

VUTHY . . . . .Joyee Lin

HAN . . . . .Tim Chiou

RA . . . . .Jennifer Shin

YEAR ZERO was produced at 2econd Stage (Carole Rothman, Artistic Director; Christopher Burney; Curator/Associate Artistic Director) at the McGinn/Cazale Theatre in New York City in June 2010. The performance was directed by Will Frears, with sets by Robin Vest, costumes by Jenny Mannis, lighting by David Weiner, and sound by M.L. Dogg. The production stage manager was Lori Ann Zepp. The cast was as follows:

GLENN . . . . Peter Kim

VUTHY . . . . .Mason Lee

HAN . . . . Louis Ozawa Changchien

RA . . . . .Maureen Sebastian

CHARACTERS

GLENN
VUTHY
HAN
RA

SETTING

Long Beach, California

TIME

Spring, 2003

Special thanks to Kimhouy Tong.

Our revenge will be the laughter of our children.

— Bobby Sands

ACT ONE

(Long Beach, California. Spring, 2003. Summer is encroaching. The air is thick with heat.)

(The kitchen and living room of a small two bedroom apartment. Old couch, old appliances. A kitchen table, chairs, a small television set.)

(Two doors lead to bedrooms. A door goes to a bathroom. A screen on the usually-open front door keeps the flies out.)

(Around the room are shelves, upon which are arranged a massive collection of objects. These can be anything small, beautiful and fragile: Glass figurines of goldfish, porcelain figures of children playing, ceramic birds. They are not chintzy or kitschy – someone collected them, displayed them like treasures, loved them.)

(There are a lot of them. Dozens is fine, hundreds would be fantastic. Their presence is the primary feature of this room.)

Scene One

(Late at night.)

*(***VUTHY** [pronounced* Woo-Tee*], 16, Cambodian American, sits at the kitchen table. He is small, wiry-skinny, weird-looking. He has thick-ass glasses that look like they keep him from blowing away.)*

(He is facing a small human skull sitting on the table. He speaks to it:)

VUTHY. See, I told you you'd like it here. You didn't want to come at first, but see? Long Beach is all right. It ain't got that humid air that you're used to, but that's OK. It's good to keep cool.

So. I gotta ask you a favor. It's a big one, so I got an offering for you: I wrote you some lyrics. I hope you like them. I wrote them for you.

*(***VUTHY** *unfolds a piece of paper. He hits play on a tape recorder. It begins playing a recording of himself beatboxing.)*

(to this he spits the following lyrics:)

I write lyrics like a Rasta rolls joints
Fools keep attackin / Tryin to take my hit points
I need more lives / Insert more coins
I'm improbable like Louis Farrakhan eatin a pork loin

Not afraid of death / Let me be a new man
Passin all your tests / Smart like a Vulcan
I break your choke hold / Give you a body slam
You chase me with your nose like you was Toucan Sam

I'm being run down / Always put upon
I'm put together well like my name was Voltron
I ride off in the snow on the back of a Tauntaun
With the devil yellin after me
Like Kirk is screaming KHAAAAAN

VUTHY. *(cont.)*

    I live my life out
    Squeezin out the most
    Eatin all my toast
    Cause all I see is ghosts
    Everywhere I look, all I see is ghosts
    All around me up in here, all I see is ghosts

(He stops the tape.)

I hope you like that. I wrote it over two trips comin back on the bus.

(beat)

So here's the favor I gotta ask you: my ma is comin' towards you, runnin' towards you. When you find her, keep her safe, take care of her. Lead her to our ancestors. Her name is Chea Vichea (*pron:* Chay Vee-Chiah), and she is my ma.

*(**VUTHY** hides the skull in a cookie jar, places it back in its home above the refrigerator.)*

Scene Two

(Morning.)

*(***VUTHY*** *eats cereal while putting the finishing touches on some homework.)*

*(***RA***, 22, his sister, comes out of the master bedroom. She is pretty in an academic way. She is carrying a basket of dirty laundry.)*

RA. You're still here.

VUTHY. The bus don't leave til seven thirty five.

RA. You'd better not miss it.

VUTHY. I won't.

RA. You better not –

VUTHY. Well, I got a bowl of imitation Froot Loops that I wanna finish eating in silence.

RA. Where'd Ma keep the quarters.

*(***VUTHY*** *points.* ***RA*** *searches through a jar of change.)*

VUTHY. On the TV news they showed Angelina Jolie in Cambodia. She was blowin' up a landmine.

RA. Good for her.

VUTHY. She was in Samlot. You think Ma ever went to Samlot?

RA. I don't know.

VUTHY. You think Ma woulda ever wanted to go back an visit?

RA. I don't know, Vuthy. How would I know that?

VUTHY. I doan know.

*(***RA*** *puts down the jar. No quarters.)*

RA. You need anything washed?

VUTHY. No.

RA. You better not be wearing your last pair of underwear –

VUTHY. IT'S NOT MY –

RA. 'Cause I only got enough quarters for one load –

VUTHY. I got enough jockies to last through the rest of tha week –

RA. You're probably wearing them twice.

VUTHY. I told you I stopped doing that –

RA. Did you remember to put on your deodorant today?

VUTHY. I got the Post It note on my mirror that reminds me to – *DANG.*

RA. It's just that girls don't like smelly boys.

VUTHY. I fuckin' know that. *Shit.*

RA. You talked like this in fronta Ma?

VUTHY. NO. You agitate me.

(**RA** *puts the laundry down by the front door, gathers flat and empty cardboard boxes.*)

RA. You better be right home after school –

VUTHY. "You better you better" –

RA. The boxes are here, okay? Soon as you get back, you start packing. We've got to be out of here in a week. And tomorrow – are you listening? – we're gonna start taking your stuff over to Aunt Tizz's. Okay?

VUTHY. She ain't even our aunt.

RA. You know how much of a big heart she's got to open up her home to you?

VUTHY. She ain't even related to us. She's just a lady that Ma used to play cards with.

RA. Well you better be nice to her.

(*She picks up the laundry, opens the front door – *)

RA. She's really doing us a favor.

VUTHY. Hey you know I heard they got this real great comic book store in Berkeley –

RA. I already talked to you about this –

VUTHY. That's run by this beardo thass-all Nazi with the comics, and in there it's like a museum of art-Fort-Knox. He got the 1940 All American with the first appearance of the Green Lantern under glass. An if the beardo doan like how you look he hits a button and it lowers into a subterranean vault –

RA. It's the middle of the school year.

VUTHY. So what?

RA. So it would be bad to move you right now, put you in a brand new school –

VUTHY. So what.

RA. So you gotta stay here with Aunt Tizz.

VUTHY. I don't care if I move, Ra. I wanna move. They hate me at Lakewood High. I almost got shivved last month –

RA. Shivved?

VUTHY. Justin Vu tried to stab me with an extra-sharp pencil. And if I had just one more inch on my waist it woulda gored me in tha flesh.

RA. Why don't you tell the Principal?

VUTHY. What's that gonna do, Ra? These kids, they doan operate under the rule of laws. They Chaotic Evil.

RA. You have friends, don't you?

VUTHY. Bert moved.

RA. What?

VUTHY. Bert. My friend. Moved to Baltimore. And I'm too Cambodian for the black and Latin kids and I'm not Cambodian enough for the Cambodian kids.

RA. What does that mean?

VUTHY. *Look at me,* Ra. I doan look normal.

RA. *(laughing)* You look fine.

VUTHY. They all got this mad dogg stare down – this whatchoo-lookin-at-sucka stare. But whenever I do it my gently arching eyebrows betray me.

RA. Look: My place in Berkeley's just one bedroom and a microwave. We have a futon for a couch –

VUTHY. I can sleep on a futon. When you get up in the morning I'll have it all put back the way it's supposed to be –

RA. Vuthy –

VUTHY. You won't even know I'm there.

RA. There's stuff all over the place – Glenn's got all his things packed in there –

VUTHY. So maybe we can get a different place – a bigger place – I can work after school, chip in –

RA. No. I'm sorry. You've just gotta be patient, okay? It's only two more years 'til you graduate. Then you'll be in college and you won't need me.

(VUTHY stares at his cereal.)

(RA picks up the laundry, opens the front door.)

RA. Remember: When you get home, start packing. We've got to be out of here in a week.

(She starts to head out –)

VUTHY. Just so you know I gotta help Om Sang move a mattress up from the storage room.

RA. Well, you do that but afterwards you gotta pack.

VUTHY. I don't know if he told you, but they're lettin Han out today.

(She pauses in the doorway.)

RA. Oh yeah?

VUTHY. Yeah. They're lettin him out of the pen. Om Sang's pickin him up this afternoon.

RA. He's getting out of prison?

VUTHY. Yeah. They're setting up his old bed next door. You didn't know that?

RA. I haven't talked to the neighbors. Haven't been keeping up on things like that.

VUTHY. *(grins)* You used to.

RA. Uh-huh. Well, if you see him, say hi to him for me.

VUTHY. He'll probably stop by. Probably want to see you. *Definitely* want to see you.

RA. Quit grinning at me and eat your cereal.

(She exits.)

VUTHY. Bus ain't here for a while still. Gots plenty of time to savor the flavor of imitation Froot.

Scene Three

(That afternoon. The apartment.)

*(**RA** wraps bowls and glasses in newspaper, carefully placing them in a box.)*

*(**HAN**, mid-20s, Cambodian American, sits at the kitchen table. He is tall, muscular, tattooed. Effortlessly handsome. He smokes, watches her.)*

RA. How's your Pa?

HAN. A'ight.

RA. "A'ight," huh?

HAN. He likes watchin TV and thass about it.

RA. Stopped by the other day with some cookies.

HAN. Yeah, he said that. Thank you.

> *(short pause)*

> You look good.

> *(She puts an ash tray out on the kitchen table.)*

RA. *(Re: the ashtray)* So you can stop using that wet paper towel.

HAN. Thanks.

RA. I'm not dumping that out for you by the way.

> *(short pause)*

HAN. How's college?

RA. Eh – I don't know. I'm three weeks behind everybody by now. They probably want to fire me at work.
How was prison?

HAN. *(smiles)* Fulla angry fools.

RA. They let you out though.

HAN. I'm not so angry anymore.
There's a "Welcome Home" party at Eddie Diep's tonight if you wanna go –

RA. With all your TRG gangster friends there? I don't think so.

HAN. If you said yes I woulda been surprised.

RA. You don't have to hang out with those guys, you know.

HAN. I'm the guest of honor. I don't got a choice.

(He holds up an MCAT study book.)

"MCAT Success."

RA. Yet another thing I'm neglecting.

HAN. It's good that you're following through with that though. It's a hard road.

RA. I guess.

HAN. I always knew you'd be up in that. You was always that type.

RA. What type is that?

HAN. Wholesome.

RA. *(laughs)* Not always.

HAN. *(smiles)* Mostly wholesome.

(short pause)

RA. So you got a job yet?

HAN. Yeah. I'm doin what every Khmer's *(pronunciation of "Khmer": KA-MAI.)* out there doin:

RA & HAN. *(together)* Makin donuts.

HAN. Yeah. Just got hired at Misty's on Atlantic.

RA. Funny how every donut shop in Long Beach is owned by Cambodians.

HAN. Well, it all started with that one guy, right? He opens a donut shop, blows up, franchises it, gets rich... Soon everybody's makin donuts.

Good thing he didn't get rich cleanin septic tanks.

RA. So are you all right working there?

HAN. I'm used to gettin up early so it'll be no problem. Come in between six and twelve. I'll hook you up with a dozen.

RA. Thanks.

(short pause)

HAN. Passed by your Ma's store. Feel bad seein it closed up.

RA. Landlord's been hassling me for the rent for next month even though he already leased it to someone else. And I still gotta sell off the rest of the inventory in there. Half a rack of chewing gum and three month old porno mags –

HAN. Guys like to jerk it to whatever's fresh.

RA. Cute.

HAN. Tell me what you got and I'll help you find buyers.

RA. Well, everything perishable has perished. Cigarettes are all sold, so it's mostly candy, mags and potato chips. And if you know anyone that's interested in a used tortilla maker, let me know.

HAN. Okay.

(beat)

Your Ma always made the best burritos.

(RA laughs.)

You know that, right? Even better than the Mexicans.

RA. High praise.

HAN. No shit. Mexicans cook everything in this city – you go into a restaurant and you'll find them makin sushi n' shit. But your Ma made the best tortas in LB. Mexicans lined up around the block for food from her store.

RA. The secret was lard.

HAN. I call that "home-style cookin."

(beat)

Four o'clock every day I'd help her lug stuff in from the back. Thass how I grew these:

(He flexes a bicep.)

Just from liftin milk.

(She flexes a bicep as well –)

RA. Well, I got em too.

HAN. *(amused)* Yeah…

After your pa passed away, she ran that place by herself. Five AM to ten at night, right?

RA. Well, the tortilla maker's there if you know anybody that wants it.

HAN. I'll put an ear out.

(She closes up a box, tapes it shut.)

You need anything? More boxes?

RA. I could use more time. So if you've got control over the time/space continuum, pull a lever or something. Otherwise –

(He takes out a thick envelope, puts it on the table.)

What's that supposed to be?

HAN. It's from the tooth fairy.

RA. Uh-huh.

HAN. To cover incidentals.

RA. Your bonus for making a record number of donuts?

HAN. Sure. Take it.

RA. I don't need it.

HAN. It's to pay your ma back.

RA. For what.

HAN. When I was little and there was nothing in our kitchen except taco shells and chocolate syrup, she'd feed me. She didn't have the money to, but she did. Can't count how many dinners she fed me. Gotta pay her back –

RA. It's all right –

HAN. And I wasn't there – at the temple, for her funeral. And I shoulda been –

RA. Keep your money.

HAN. I owe your ma.

(He pushes the money toward her.)

And so you don't have to worry.

(She takes the money, holds it out to him –)

RA. I don't want it.

(She tosses it onto the table in front of him.)

I'm doing all right. Doing fine.

(A pause. He watches her work.)

(VUTHY *enters through the front door. There's blood on his shirt. He has the makings of a bad black eye.)*

VUTHY. *(re:* **HAN***)* It's him: The world's largest Cambodian!

HAN. Vuthy!

(HAN *hugs him.)*

I ain't even that big.

VUTHY. Well, we are, by nature, a smallish people.

(HAN *weighs* **VUTHY***'s head in his hands.)*

HAN. Your head's still the heaviest part of your body.

VUTHY. You still need help gettin your mattress?

HAN. Nah, we got it –

(beat)

What happened to your eye?

VUTHY. Samoans.

RA. What do you mean "Samoans"?

VUTHY. I saved up my lunch money to get some cheeseburgers at Mac Donalds after school. And I was waitin for the bus when these Samoans – linebacker, hill-sized muthafuckahs – came up on me and was like, "Whatchoo got in that MAG-Donalds bag?" "Nothin," I said. And then they said "Gimme your bag fulla nothin!" and then they popped me. Gots beat up over a cheeseburger.

(She dabs at his face with a dish rag.)

RA. Why didn't you just give them the food?

VUTHY. I know these Samoans. They was gonna pop me anyways. Thought I could make it through with the cheeseburgers intact.

HAN. You should've hit them.

RA. NO, he shouldn't have.

VUTHY. These Samoans hit real hard – they got a lotta upper body strength. Must be from all the paddlin.

RA. They go to your school?

VUTHY. Yeah.

RA. Okay, now we're really gonna go to the Principal.

HAN. Thass not gonna do anything –

RA. Will you please shut up?

> *(She examines **VUTHY**'s face, dabs at it with a paper towel –)*

There's a cut here – you're bleeding over your eye –

VUTHY. It doan hurt anymore. OW!

RA. You're lucky you don't need stitches –

VUTHY. You know, I betchu that there's no Samoans in Berkeley.

RA. No, I'm pretty sure that there are.

VUTHY. Yeah but I bet they ain't the kind that steals peoples' Mac Donalds –

> *(**VUTHY** spots **HAN**'s cigarettes –)*

VUTHY. Teach me how to smoke!

HAN. Okay.

RA. NO.

> *(She grabs **VUTHY** by the arm, drags him to the bathroom –)*

We've got to wash this out, put a band-aid over it –

VUTHY. *(to **HAN**:)* You gonna stay for a while, right? I got the new X-Men I wanna show you.

> *(**HAN** stands, picks up his things.)*

HAN. Got some things I gotta do. Knock on our door later tonight.

VUTHY. A'ight. Bye –

> *(**RA** drags **VUTHY** into the bathroom to clean him up – we can hear them squabbling from off.)*
>
> *(**HAN** puts out his cigarette, dumps out the ashtray.)*
>
> *(And he hides the envelope of money in one of **RA**'s moving boxes.)*

Scene Four

*(**HAN**'s car.)*

*(**HAN** drives. **VUTHY** watches the world float by the passenger's window.)*

(On the radio:)

GEORGE W. BUSH. Admiral Kelly, Captain Card, officers and sailors of the USS Abraham Lincoln, my fellow Americans: Major combat operations in Iraq have ended. In the battle of Iraq, the United States and our allies have prevailed –

HAN. Fuck that motherfucker. Fuckin Saddam Hussein. Motherfucka gasses his own people. I hope they find him and ghost his ass.

VUTHY. Me too.

HAN. Four years ago, when my pa still had his store, George W. Bush stopped by while he was campaigning. Didja know that, Vuthy?

VUTHY. Naw, really?

HAN. Yeah. Bought a Twix and shook my hand. When nobody wanted us, Ronald Reagan let us into this country.

VUTHY. I know.

HAN. Never forget that, Vuthy.

VUTHY. I won't.

Thanks for takin me to school.

HAN. Yeah, don't worry about it. You get good grades?

VUTHY. "A"s except for P.E.

HAN. Juss do what the teacher tells you and he won't be able to give you nothing less than an A.

(short pause)

So Ra said you went back to tha motherland over the summer.

VUTHY. Yeah. The temple sponsored a group trip back to Cambodia.

HAN. How'd you like it?

VUTHY. It's hot, man – hot and moist. And the people over there is *dark*. Mahogany brown.

HAN. Well, you and your sister got a lotta Chinese in you.

VUTHY. They got these Happy Pizzas –

HAN. Oh yeah. I heard about those.

VUTHY. Yeah, with the weed baked in the cheese.

HAN. *(laughs) Chronic pizzas.* You eat one?

VUTHY. No, but Peter Meang did. He thought monkeys were gonna jump outta the trees and steal his eyebrows.

HAN. Where else you go?

VUTHY. Angkor Wat. With the trees growing out of the stones…makes you feel small. To know that so many people lived before you did.

HAN. We are the sons of Kings. Don't forget that, Vuthy.

VUTHY. I won't.

HAN. You go to Tuol Sleng, Choeung Ek, (*Pron:* Tull Slang, Chung Ech) any of those places?

VUTHY. The Killing Fields –

HAN. Yeah –

VUTHY. Yeah, in Cheoung Ek they had this temple in the middle of the field. And inside they had these racks of skulls from all the people the Khmer Rouge killed, hundreds of em, right out there in fronta you – so close you could touch 'em.

HAN. Yeah?

VUTHY. You could grab one, throw it in your backpack if you really wanted to.

(beat)

You think you'll ever go back there again?

HAN. Naw. Don't need to see that. Glad you got to though. Every Khmer man needs to know where he comes from.

VUTHY. I didn't wanna go at first. But Ma really wanted me
    to. I feel good that I did.

    (short pause)

HAN. So these Samoans: They pick on you a lot?

VUTHY. Sometimes. I doan know.

HAN. You gotta stick with your own kind, Vuthy: Khmer
    people.

VUTHY. Yeah, but it seems that the Khmer kids are the most
    interested in beatin me up.

HAN. What?
    Why is that?

VUTHY. I dunno. Doan matter anyway. Somebody's gotta
    get beat up.

HAN. Yeah, but why's that gotta be you?

VUTHY. While it's happening I tell myself that it builds
    character.

HAN. Naw, Vuthy – that ain't right.
    Next time one of these motherfuckers comes up on
    you, do me a favor: Fuckin hit em. Hit em as hard as
    you can with whatever you got, you feel me?

VUTHY. *(unsure about this)* Yeah –

HAN. Listen: You know why the yin-yang has a dot of black
    in the middle of the white circle and a dot of white in
    the middle of the black circle?

VUTHY. Why?

HAN. 'Cause inside everything is a tiny core of its oppo-
    site. Inside the strongest, baddest motherfucka in the
    world is a core of weakness. So if someone big and bad
    fucks with you, don't even think about it: Hit em as
    hard as you can. Fucks 'em up. Shakes 'em to the core.

VUTHY. Okay, Han.

HAN. Okay.
    Your ma know you got beat up so much?

VUTHY. Naw. Didn't wanna worry her.

HAN. Okay. Thass good.

VUTHY. Maybe...I should join TRG. Like you. You high up in there – maybe you could put in a good word for me –

HAN. Thass not for you. TRG is for guys that don't got families. TRG is their family. But you – you just gotta man up a little.

VUTHY. The thing is, I'm not exactly sure how to do that.

HAN. Well, that may be something we can do somethin about.

(beat)

So what's up with your sis?... That punk she shackin with in Nor Cal –

VUTHY. "Glenn."

HAN. Yeah. How long they been together?

VUTHY. I doan know. Two years now?... I fuckin hate that guy. Last time I seen him he's like, "Hey Vuthy why don't you try playin' tennis?..." Tennis? Do I look like I'm in a country club? Fuckin thirsty-ass, Orange County motherfucker.

(HAN laughs.)

HAN. So what you gonna do when Ra goes back up there?

VUTHY. Stay here with Aunt Tizz.

HAN. You really wanna do that?

VUTHY. I doan know.

HAN. She nice, but it smells like moth balls and cat piss over there.

VUTHY. I know.

HAN. Well maybe we can figure something else out.

VUTHY. Really?

HAN. Yeah.

(He pulls the car over.)

Okay. I'll pick you up at three fifteen, on this spot.

VUTHY. Okay. Hey –

HAN. What.

VUTHY. Thanks for comin back.

Scene Five

(The apartment. That afternoon.)

(VUTHY is sitting at the kitchen table. Dungeons and Dragons character sheets, reference books, and various types of dice are spread out on the table.)

(He's playing Dungeons and Dragons on the phone:)

VUTHY. So you're at a fork in the passageway. Do you wanna go left or right?... Okay, you point Hrogg's Decapitated Head left. Its eyes glow red, lighting the dark passage ahead. Yeah. Okay, you go left... You enter a huge cavern, and then you see it: An ORC encampment – tents, warthogs roastin on spits, Orcish weapons in stacks – and all around are dozens of Orcs kickin it doin Orc things. Crackin jokes, tellin Orc stories. This they crib.

(laughs)

Yeah, they drinkin Orc ale from Orc forties. You're fuckin funny, Bert!

(beat)

Okay – you try to sneak up to them –

(VUTHY rolls a D20.)

But they see you. SHIT! They mobbin you – mad doggin you. And they see you got Hrogg's Decapitated Head and they pissed! They fuckin pissed! ...And the strongest, baddest one of them comes up on you and is like, "Yo, you got Hrogg's fuckin head – you kilt him! You fuckin kilt my homie?!" So what do you do –

(There's a knock at the screen door.)

(into the phone:)

Hold on.

(GLENN, mid-20s, Chinese American, peeks his head in. He is good looking, clean cut, preppy.)

GLENN. Anybody home?

(**VUTHY** *focuses his stare on* **GLENN** *as he enters.*)

Hey Vuthy. How's it going?

VUTHY. I'm DM'ing right now.

GLENN. Oh yeah, neat. Is Ra here?

VUTHY. She's out.

GLENN. Oh. Well, I came down to surprise her.

VUTHY. Well, the effect of that's kinda lost 'cause she's out.

GLENN. Okay. So – is it okay if I wait here?

(**VUTHY** *stares at him.*)

Hey – when I was exiting the freeway I noticed that there's a mall. Do you know if there's a Banana Republic there? I gotta return some stuff –

VUTHY. Do I look like I know the answer to that question, Glenn?

GLENN. Okay. Well, I'm going to the mall then.
You wanna come with?

(**VUTHY** *doesn't respond.*)

Okay. Can I leave my stuff here?

(*Still no response.*)

Well, tell your sister I'm here, and… "Surprise."

VUTHY. Yay.

(**GLENN** *exits out the front door.*)

Thirsty-ass mother…

(*back on the phone:*)

Sorry, dude. Okay, so what do you do?… A'ight, you draw your sword – and the motherfucka's like, "Whoa, whoa…"

Scene Six

(The apartment. Later that afternoon.)

(HAN is cooking on the stove. RA leans against the counter, watching him.)

HAN. Thanks for this. Chelly don't have time to fix my pa's stove till Monday.

RA. Sure, it's no problem. What is that?

HAN. Ox tails. Just need to warm 'em.

RA. Smells good.

HAN. A little garlic powder. Kicks it up.

RA. Thanks for picking Vuthy up from school.

HAN. You're welcome.

So he say that after you're gone he gonna stay with Aunt Tizz.

RA. That's right.

HAN. Okay, 'cause you know he can stay with me and my pa –

RA. No way.

HAN. Why no way.

RA. You know why.

HAN. Hah.

RA. You know that if you get in trouble again, they can deport you. Right?

HAN. Uh-huh.

RA. "Cambodia wants its sons back."

HAN. Well. Makin donuts in Cambodia don't sound so bad.

RA. It's not funny. It happens. Bobby Moeuk: They got him on breaking and entering, sent him to jail. Selling stolen parts offa Civics, sent him to jail. Then they take him in for unpaid parking tickets: Boom – deported back to Cambodia. For unpaid parking tickets.

HAN. I'm careful.

RA. Says the guy who just got outta prison.

HAN. I'm careful *now*.

RA. I'm not some dumb teenage girl anymore. I know what you are. In high school, those TRG girls with the crispy hair and talon-like nails – they all knew your name.

(**HAN** *laughs, stirs the ox tails.*)

I know who your friends are. Where you get your money. That boy of yours – Donny: Donny Neak –

HAN. Uh-huh –

RA. With the Acura Integra he paid for in hundred dollar bills –

HAN. We knew a guy at the dealership that cut him a deal for cash.

RA. Right. Your partner in crime: Donny Neak. Stabbed that kid in the chest three times –

HAN. The kid wasn't hurt – the knife kept bouncin off his rib cage –

RA. Sure.

So once he gets out of prison, you two gonna be Bonnie and Clyde again?

HAN. (*a beat, thinking:*) Don't worry about Donny. I can handle Donny.

(*short pause*)

RA. Taking Vuthy to school, picking him up: That's okay. But if you really wanna help him out, leave it at that.

HAN. So why you not takin him with you?

RA. This is only temporary. I'm giving Aunt Tizz a few hundred bucks a month to help out –

HAN. A'ight...

RA. So thank you for offering, but I made arrangements already.

HAN. And anyway, you got the MCATs now. And that dude, Glenn –

RA. Yes, Glenn. So if you're on my case about him, too –

HAN. No. That's cool that you got somebody.

RA. Fine.

(RA unfolds a cardboard box, tapes its bottom solid.)

RA. *(cont.)* I've gotta get back to school – and I'm sorry, I wish I could take him, but we don't have the room and I don't have the time.

HAN. Okay. You don't haveta explain it to me.

RA. Good, because I'm not going to anymore.

And I've only got a few days left to pack up the rest of this room, and as you can see, I've got a lot of work to do –

(Re: Ma's objects)

I don't know what the hell I'm gonna do with these things.

HAN. Your Ma sure loved them.

RA. I don't even know where she got them. Every week or so she'd come home with a new one, add it to the shelf. I told her not to waste money on them. "Stop bringing those home," I told her. We're gonna drown in them.

HAN. She said she liked lookin at them. It made her happy to see all of them together. Like little people in little rows lookin back at her.

RA. She told you that?

HAN. Yeah.

RA. I never heard her say that.

HAN. She told that to me every now and then.

(He scans the shelves of objects, finds a particular one that is seemingly indistinguishable from the others:)

Hah – here it is.

This is it.

RA. What.

(He grabs it, shows it to her.)

HAN. This is the first one.

RA. What do you mean?

HAN. This is the one she brought with her when she came here. The one from Cambodia.

RA. What?

HAN. She had it when she was little. She carried it with her everywhere. When the Khmer Rouge took her family… When she escaped. And even when she came here.

(beat)

This is the first one.

RA. I didn't know –

HAN. I thought you did –

RA. How come she told you this but –

HAN. I thought you –

(beat)

What did she tell you about her life back there?

RA. We never talked about it.

HAN. What?

RA. She just worked, ran her store –

HAN. Well, you know about your grandma, your grandpa, your aunts, your uncle –

RA. No. She never told me about them. All I know is that I was born there. She escaped from the Khmer Rouge, met my pa in a refugee camp in Thailand, and that's it.

HAN. They was gonna kill your uncle 'cause he had glasses. They killed people with glasses, 'cause if you're smart, you gonna rise up.

So your uncle had to throw em away.

Every day they'd walk from the huts where they slept to the fields where they made 'em work, and he'd hold on to your Ma by the shoulder –

And one day this Khmer Rouge soldier comes up on him and is like, "How many fingers am I holding up?" And your Ma, right, she was standing close by and tapped your uncle four times.

(He pauses, reflecting on this.)

She usedta tell me things all the time. Stories about your grandma and grandpa's farm –

(beat)

I'm surprised that she didn't –

RA. Well, I asked her once: "Ma, what happened back there?" You know what she said? "Have you finished studying yet? Have you eaten yet?"

So I didn't ask again.

HAN. Well, I guess some things hurt to tell. And what happened back there –

RA. She told you.

HAN. Because I wasn't one of her kids. Because I was there when I was little – 'cause I had seen some of those things, too.

(beat)

I wish she had told you, Ra –

RA. Well, she didn't.

HAN. Because those things – those stories...

(beat)

Before you go, if –

RA. Hey – I've gotta go down to the store, pick up some stuff. Eggs, cereal – you need anything?

HAN. No, I'll –

*(**RA** grabs her things –)*

RA. Okay –

HAN. You want me to come with you?

RA. No. Just let yourself out. Okay?

(He studies her for a moment.)

HAN. Yeah.

(She exits.)

(He watches her go.)

(Then he carefully places the first object back in its home among the shelves.)

Scene Seven

(The apartment. Night.)

*(**RA** sits alone, trying to study.)*

*(**GLENN** enters through the front door carrying cartons of food.)*

GLENN. I'm back.

(He begins to unpack the food.)

RA. Are you sure your attending is okay letting you come down here?

GLENN. Roger's fine with it. I brought my computer. Got a bunch of studies to do.

(He offers her a carton:)

Kung-Pao Chicken!

(beat)

He would've been looking over my shoulder anyway, nit-picking every dictation I do.

RA. Uh-huh.

GLENN. But I'm in good shape – Roger can email me any studies I need to view, so don't worry – I'm all set.

(He notices the MCAT book.)

I'm glad to see that you're still enthralled with the field of medicine.

RA. Don't worry – all the excitement's been sucked out of me.

GLENN. Just wait 'til you get into med school. "The most efficient ass kicking – "

RA. *(overlapping)* " – Machine devised by man."

GLENN. But I know you:

(He kisses her on the top of the head.)

Keep grittin your teeth.

You'll make it.

(He puts out three table settings.)

I've been meaning to ask you: How was the funeral?

RA. It was a funeral. Small, quiet, over with.

GLENN. Ra, I'm sorry that –

RA. I already told you: You don't have to apologize, and you didn't have to be there.

GLENN. I know, but… She was your mother, Ra. You said not to come, but I should've come anyway.

I should've been there at the temple with you.

RA. Forget it. Don't mention it. Seriously.

GLENN. I know you miss her.

RA. Well what can you do.

(He sits with her.)

GLENN. I came down because I wanted to see how you're doing –

RA. I'm fine –

GLENN. And I missed you. Turns out I don't like sleeping alone –

RA. Sure. Every night you come home at one a.m., jump into bed, go into a coma. Like you even notice I'm there.

GLENN. Well, now that you're gone I definitely feel your omission.

RA. So you liken me to a mistake on an essay.

GLENN. *(laughs)* Supremely bad choice of words. But I needed to see you.

RA. Uh-huh.

GLENN. I mean, in a couple years we're getting married, right?

(She shows him her hand.)

RA. That's funny, I don't see a ring here.

GLENN. Because the time isn't right.

RA. Ah yes. The time.

(beat)

It's not your family. It's not because I'm Cambodian and –

GLENN. *(laughs)* Okay: That has nothing to do with this.

RA. Where exactly are we on the Asian hierarchy? Below Vietnamese, above – I don't know – Orangutans?

GLENN. Chinese, Vietnamese, Orangutans, Cambodians, Pandas.

RA. Hah.

GLENN. And what they think has got nothing to do with this, Ra. Radiology: I'm sitting in the dark in front of a PACS machine sixteen hours a day –

RA. Uh-huh –

GLENN. I've got to put together a little stability, first. Okay?

(beat)

But I'm here now with some beef and broccoli, and it's all for you.

(HAN and VUTHY enter through the screen door.)

(VUTHY makes a beeline for his room –)

RA. Halt –

VUTHY. Already ate.

GLENN. I brought Chinese food!

VUTHY. Way to reinforce a stereotype, Glenn.

RA. *(to VUTHY:)* Where are you going?

VUTHY. Gotta get online to see if Bert's sent me an email.

RA. Don't tie up the phone.

VUTHY. Geez, I won't.

(He disappears into his room.)

(HAN hovers over the table.)

RA. Glenn, this is Han.

GLENN. Sup.

(GLENN offers a fist. HAN looks at it amused, then pounds it.)

HAN. Sup. So you're Glenn, huh? Heard a lot about you.

GLENN. My reputation precedes. And you are –

HAN. The neighbor's kid.

GLENN. Kinda large to be a kid, aren't you?

HAN. Roids.

(**GLENN** *pauses over this, then laughs –*)

Nah, I juss lift a lot.

GLENN. Cool, cool. How much do you bench?

(**HAN** *remains silent, amused.*)

You hungry?

HAN. We got Roscoe's earlier.

GLENN. Oh yeah – the famous chicken and waffles, right?

RA. Delicious.

GLENN. We'll have to check that out before we leave.

HAN. I'm picking Vuthy up in an hour. Check out a movie.

RA. Just you and Vuthy?

HAN. Just me and Vuthy.

RA. Okay. Fine.

HAN. A'ight then. See ya later, big man.

GLENN. *(playful)* Holler.

(**HAN** *exits out the front door.*)

The neighbor's kid, huh?

RA. Yup.

GLENN. He was ripped. When he said 'roids I didn't know
    if he was kidding.

(**RA** *knocks on* **VUTHY***'s door.*)

(**VUTHY** *pops his head out –*)

VUTHY. What.

RA. What movie are you gonna see.

VUTHY. Huh?

RA. What movie.

VUTHY. The Matrix 2.

RA. Okay. When it's over you come right back here. No
    hanging out with Han and his friends –

VUTHY. WHY.

RA. A normal social life is fine. But whatever those guys are
   up to is not for you.

VUTHY. Well, we was gonna rob a bank tonight but I guess
   thass off the agenda –

   (**GLENN** *laughs.*)

RA. Shut up. Be back here by ten.

VUTHY. Eleven.

RA. Ten thirty.

VUTHY. Ten forty-five.

RA. Ten *fifteen.*

VUTHY. So it was okay for you to hang with those guys when
   you was my age but now it's not okay for me –

RA. Yes. Because Han and his friends are up to no good –

VUTHY. You should know.

RA. What's that supposed to mean?

GLENN. It's just a movie, Ra. Give the kid a break –

RA. Will you eat your egg rolls and shut the fuck up?

GLENN. Eating my egg rolls…

RA. *(beat, to* **VUTHY**, *sotto:)* When I was your age I was a
   stupid kid, Vuthy. And the reason I don't have a tod-
   dler right now is 'cause Ma kept me away from guys
   like Han.

VUTHY. Like that stopped you.

RA. You better shut up about that –

   (**VUTHY** *shrugs* **RA** *away from his door –*)

VUTHY. Stay off the phone. I gotta check the Internet.

   (*He closes his door.*)

RA. That fucking kid.

GLENN. Well, he just wants to hang out with the guys. It's
   perfectly natural.

RA. You don't know the guys around here.

Scene Eight

(Later that night. A suburban brothel.)

(A doorway with a beaded curtain, colored lights. Nearby sound of a baseball game on TV.)

(HAN walks through the beaded curtain. VUTHY pauses behind it.)

HAN. Get in here.

(HAN puts an arm through the curtain, pulls VUTHY through.)

VUTHY. Oh. Geez.

HAN. Yeah.

VUTHY. Manny Nguyen at school always said this house was a ho house. I didn't believe him.

HAN. Well, Manny Nguyen was right.

VUTHY. Thass funny – it looks just like a regular house on the outside –

HAN. Yeah, I don't know how they do that. Must be magic.

(points:)

Choose one.

VUTHY. What? …No, man – I can't –

HAN. I got you. Don't worry about it –

VUTHY. No –

HAN. Just choose one of those girls. I got you.

(VUTHY presses his face into HAN's shoulder, embarrassed –)

VUTHY. I can't, man.

HAN. Why not?

VUTHY. I'm shy.

HAN. Fuck you, you're shy. Choose one of those girls before I hit you.

(VUTHY laughs awkwardly –)

VUTHY. I've never done it before –

HAN. Thass kinda the point.

VUTHY. Han –

HAN. Choose one or I'll choose one for you.

VUTHY. This is weird.

HAN. What's weird about it? They're selling, you're buying. Look: If you don't like any of the ones here I know another place. But it's a lot more fobby –

VUTHY. Okay – okay.

(He nervously scans around.)

HAN. How 'bout her.

VUTHY. She's a little too old.

HAN. Her.

VUTHY. She looks like an alien.

HAN. Okay, her.

VUTHY. She looks too much like Ra. Oh shit – was that fucked up of me to say?

HAN. No, I feel you. How 'bout her – she's a stunner –

VUTHY. No – she's too cute. I'd nut too quick –

HAN. Thass okay. First time around, every dude lasts like five seconds. So I got you covered for two rounds. The first time, don't worry about shootin one off. Then you can relax, hit it a second time and get into it once the pressure's off –

VUTHY. What are you gonna do?

HAN. Don't worry about me. The Dodger game's on.

*(**VUTHY** spots someone on the other side of the room:)*

VUTHY. Oh shit.

HAN. What?

VUTHY. Thass Heidi Trang!

HAN. Who?

VUTHY. Heidi Trang. She was like, a senior when I was a freshman.

HAN. Oh. Yeah, Heidi.

VUTHY. Shit – she's a ho now?

HAN. Everybody got their own destination. So you wanna put your *kahldol (Pron:* kah-DAH*)* in her or what?

VUTHY. Shit, Han – I can't.

HAN. Why not?

VUTHY. She was runner up for Prom Queen –

HAN. So what?

VUTHY. Han –

HAN. Thass it – she's the one. You're doing her on principle. Don't worry, she good.

VUTHY. You? –

HAN. Yeah.

(He motions –)

Hey: Heidi! This young buck here wants to meet you.

(He takes a couple of condoms out of his pocket, hands them to **VUTHY**.*)*

Go.

*(***VUTHY*** steps forward slowly, freezes –)*

VUTHY. Han –

HAN. What now?

VUTHY. I never even… I never –

HAN. What?

VUTHY. I never even kissed a girl before.

HAN. Oh. Well, that's the one thing you can't do here: You can't kiss 'em.

(grinning)

And that's probably the only thing you can't do here. But if you want, we can probably set something up –

VUTHY. No.

HAN. No what?

VUTHY. No, that's… I wanna save that for… I want that to be special.

*(***HAN*** studies him, puzzled, then gets it.)*

HAN. Okay. No kissing then.

So go. I'll be right here.

(And **VUTHY** *steps forward into the darkness.)*

Scene Nine

(The apartment. Night.)

(GLENN throws a bedspread over the couch.)

(RA closes her MCAT book.)

RA. Don't do that – the thing's thirty years old. It's got a spring that'll go right into your shoulder blade.

GLENN. It's all right. I don't mind.

RA. Just stay with me. My Mom's bed.

GLENN. You sure that's okay?

RA. It's just a bed, Glenn.

> *(GLENN folds up the bedspread. RA reopens her book, continues studying.)*

GLENN. I never got to meet her. Your mom.

RA. Uh-huh.

GLENN. I don't think I've even seen a picture of her.

RA. There aren't many really.

GLENN. Nothing? No vacation pictures?

RA. We weren't the family vacation type.

> *(short pause)*

GLENN. How much did you tell her about us?

> *(RA puts down the book:)*

RA. Look – you know I wanna take this thing in August, right?

GLENN. Yes –

RA. I put this off and I have to put off grad apps.

GLENN. Okay –

RA. So can you just do some more dictations or watch TV or something and let me finish this section at least –

GLENN. Fine.

> *(GLENN turns on the TV, turns the volume down low. He sits, stares at it.)*

> *(RA puts her book away, sits next to him.)*

RA. I'm sorry. I'm sorry –

GLENN. It's okay. If there's any time you've got a right to be pissed for no reason, it's –

RA. Stop.

GLENN. What.

RA. Stop trying to be so fucking fair.

GLENN. *(smiles)* Done.

> *(He puts his arm around her, kisses her head.)*

I was just wondering what your mom was like. I was wondering if she was like you.

RA. I don't know –

GLENN. Was she tough like you?

RA. You think I'm tough.

GLENN. You get things done.

RA. It doesn't take guts to check shit off a to-do list.

GLENN. You know what I mean.

RA. Uh-huh.

> *(short pause)*

You know why your attending picks on you?

GLENN. Why.

RA. Because you're good.

GLENN. *(laughs)* You think so?

RA. Yeah.

GLENN. Well, then. It's good to see you, Ra.

> *(He touches her neck warmly.)*
>
> *(She touches him back. He moves closer, kisses her.)*
>
> *(And as he kisses her neck, she looks away, distant.)*

Scene Ten

(**HAN**'s car.)

(**HAN** drives. **VUTHY** stares out the passenger's window.)

HAN. How you feel?

VUTHY. I dunno. Different. A little sick.

HAN. You all right?

VUTHY. I think so.

HAN. I didn't expect you to have a good time. First time's never good. Part of becoming a man is learning how to make it good. Next time it'll be with your girl and it'll be a different sorta thing –

VUTHY. Uh-huh.

HAN. What's wrong?

VUTHY. It's kinda…sad, don't you think, that Heidi Trang is a ho now.

HAN. You feel bad for her.

VUTHY. Yeah.

HAN. Was she nice to you in school or somethin? You vote for her for Prom Queen?

VUTHY. No. I doan know.

(beat)

She had a nice smile. She didn't smile at me or nothin, but… I seen her smile before. Her eyes'd turn into little half-circles when she smiled –

HAN. How was she?

VUTHY. I doan know.

HAN. You don't have to tell me if you don't want to.

VUTHY. She was a'ight. She didn't say nothin. I think I woulda crapped my pants if she did say somethin. I was nervous –

HAN. Sure.

VUTHY. And I didn't expect her to smile, but… Her skin felt cold. Like paper. And she was thin. So thin, like her body didn't have any blood in it.

HAN. So thass why you feel bad for her?

VUTHY. Yeah.

HAN. Well, she coulda been something else, but thass what she chose. Most people ain't like you. We take the easy way out.

VUTHY. What do you mean?

HAN. It's hard to get As in everything except P.E. It's hard to draw as good as you do –

VUTHY. Huh.

HAN. What, is it easy for you? Gettin all As keeps the other kids from beatin yo ass?

VUTHY. No. It's just… I'm just wondering what Heidi's ma must be thinking. That's all.

HAN. Maybe she don't know. Or maybe she's why Heidi's there. I don't know.

VUTHY. She could get outta there if she really wanted to –

HAN. You wanna go back and save her?

VUTHY. No –

HAN. Then what, Vuthy?

VUTHY. I just feel bad for her, is all.

HAN. Well, thass her choice. Nobody chooses how they're born, but some people choose how they die.

VUTHY. You think she chose that, Han?

HAN. You haven't seen her shootin shit into her arm.

(beat)

See, you and your sister – you had something going for you. Your ma. You was lucky. Most people, Vuthy – they don't got that.

VUTHY. I know.

(short pause)

HAN. You ever ask her… You ever ask your ma about her life in Cambodia?

VUTHY. Naw. I didn't want to… She was always workin, or – you could tell she was tired from workin, and so I didn't –

HAN. A'ight.

But… If you ever got anything you wanna ask, you can ask me. 'Cause I'm back now. I'm back for good.

(short pause)

VUTHY. I heard about your friend Donny Neak.

HAN. What about him?

VUTHY. I heard they're lettin him out.

HAN. How you know about that?

VUTHY. Everybody knows.

HAN. Uh-huh. So what.

VUTHY. So what are you gonna do?

HAN. You know what I gotta do.

(short pause)

VUTHY. Why's it gotta be you?…

Why do you have to be the one?

HAN. Vuthy –

VUTHY. 'Cause I doan want you to do it –

HAN. Listen:

VUTHY. I thought you and Donny was tight –

HAN. We been friends since we was like, seven years old. We usedta have the same bowl cut. People thought we was twins.

VUTHY. Yeah, so –

HAN. And that's why, Vuthy: It has to be me.

(short pause)

VUTHY. What did Donny do? Why can't they let him go?

HAN. 'Cause he's a snitchin motherfucker who can't keep his mouth shut.

(short pause)

Don't worry about me. I'ma be all right.

I'ma still be here for you, take you to school, pick you up. You're my *phuon proh.* *(Pron:* Pa-OWN Proh, *short "O" as in "Off")* You're my brother, Vuthy. Thass not gonna change.

VUTHY. We could just keep on going. Get on the 405, you an' me –

HAN. Vuthy –

VUTHY. We could just keep going, get somewhere safe –

HAN. You wanna leave your sister alone?

VUTHY. She wants to pass me off on Aunt Tizz. She doan care.

HAN. Naw. I gotta stay. Do what I gotta do.

VUTHY. Why?

HAN. 'Cause if I don't take care of Donny, someone else will take care of me.

Scene Eleven

(The apartment. Late at night.)

*(**RA** sits in her pajamas, meticulously wrapping Ma's objects in newspaper.)*

(She wraps one and puts it in a moving box, wraps a second one. She looks at the remaining masses of them, frustrated. She picks up a third, begins to wrap it –)

(And it accidentally falls out of her hands, hits the ground.)

(She scrambles, desperately picks the fallen object up and examines it.)

(And she begins to cry.)

(She collapses, crying over the object.)

*(**HAN** watches her through the screen door, then steps through –)*

HAN. Ra –

(She straightens herself up but can't stop crying.)

Hey – it's all right –

(She stands, puts her arms around him –)

It's okay.

(He strokes her hair, holds her close.)

RA. Han –

HAN. Yeah –

RA. Tell me about my mother.

HAN. What do you want to know –

RA. Was she ever hungry? Was she ever scared?…
My aunts, my uncle – what happened to them?…What were their names?…
My grandpa, my grandma – what were they… Did any of them –

HAN. No. Your ma was the only one that –
She dug their graves.

RA. The Khmer Rouge: When she escaped –

HAN. She had no shoes.

Did you know that?

She walked hundreds of miles barefoot, by herself.

RA. Why did she –

HAN. Because she saw you in a dream. Before you were born. And that's when she knew: She had to run.

RA. Han: Did she ever...did she ever say that –

(He pauses, thinking.)

HAN. Yeah. She said it all the time, Ra: She said she loved you all the time.

(She touches his face, pulls him closer.)

(She kisses him, wraps herself up in him. She takes him by the hand –)

RA. Is your Pa asleep?

(He nods.)

(And she quietly leads him out the front door.)

End of Act One

ACT TWO

Scene One

(The apartment. Morning.)

(GLENN sits at the kitchen table over his open laptop.)

(He speaks into a small recording device:)

GLENN. Patient is a forty-five year-old male, presents with numbness in the face and right leg weakness. MR angiography of the neck reveals a focal stenosis of the origin of the left internal carotid artery amounting to… Fifty percent stenosis –

(VUTHY comes out of his bedroom, pours himself a bowl of imitation Froot Loops.)

(continuing as he watches VUTHY)

The remainder of the left carotid circulation is unremarkable. On the right side there is a twenty percent stenosis of the origin of the right internal carotid artery. The vertebral and basilar arteries are unremarkable –

(VUTHY heads back toward his room.)

(GLENN snaps off the recording device.)

Hey, have you seen your sister?

VUTHY. Nope.

GLENN. She wasn't here this morning.

VUTHY. Maybe she went to the store.

GLENN. I gotta go to the library, use the high speed internet – could you tell her that I'll be back this afternoon –

VUTHY. Well, I gotta go to GameStop, so why don't you send her a fuckin email?

GLENN. I'll write her a note.

(GLENN *pulls out a chair for* VUTHY. VUTHY *doesn't sit.*)

She said that you want to become a comic book artist.

VUTHY. Graphic novels.

GLENN. Graphic novels, then.

VUTHY. And?

GLENN. She said that you like Superman.

(GLENN *produces a comic book in a plastic wrapper.*)

Don't know if you have this one. It's the one where Supes dies.

(VUTHY *examines it.*)

I've had it for a while. I used to follow the book pretty hardcore, but I thought that was a good place to stop. I thought you might like it.

(*beat*)

Superman's actually the quintessential immigrant story.

VUTHY. What now?

GLENN. He's the consummate immigrant. Born by another name on an alien planet, the first generation of his family to arrive on earth. He comes to America, flourishes here because of our warm yellow sun. He discovers new powers. He acclimatizes, but he always has two separate identities. One of them he keeps secret. And whenever he encounters a piece of his home world, it's harmful to him. You know what I mean? ...The story of Superman is the story of immigrants in America.

VUTHY. Huh. Well you forgot something: Superman is white. You think that IF, in 1938, an Asian baby crashed by the sidea the road Ma and Pa Kent woulda taken him in? No fuckin way. They woulda called up Smallville Social Services. Had his ass picked up. Kal-El woulda growed up in a group home.

GLENN. You're probably right.

(VUTHY pushes the comic book back across the table.)

VUTHY. Keep your comic book.

(VUTHY heads toward his room.)

GLENN. Hey, if you're hungry I brought you back an Egg McMuffin –

VUTHY. FUCK YOU.

GLENN. What's your fucking problem?

VUTHY. You're my fuckin problem, Glennnnnnn –

GLENN. What did I do to you?

VUTHY. Well you got two 'N's in your name and thass annoying as fuck.

GLENN. Okay: Let's just get this out there – you hate me because I'm sleeping with your sister –

VUTHY. Oh fuck, you went there.

GLENN. I'd be pissed too, all right? So I'm rationalizing it to myself like this: what you're doing is perfectly natural –

VUTHY. Okay, good –

GLENN. And I'm trying to be nice to you. And I'm trying to see things from your viewpoint –

VUTHY. Well, now that thass out of the way, let's be homies –

GLENN. But when does this stop? Seriously.
   Because it's stupid, okay? Because when it comes down to it, you and I are so much alike –

VUTHY. Oh, don't tell me that shit Glenn.

GLENN. No, listen –

VUTHY. Because we're not. Now why don't you jump in your Audi and go buy some fuckin slacks.

GLENN. I was legally blind.

VUTHY. What?

GLENN. I used to have these thick-ass glasses, used to read everything like this –

(He holds a piece of paper three inches away from his face –)

GLENN. *(cont.)* Which was not very popular with the ladies, as you can imagine – uhmmm… And I was your physical opposite: I was a blob. You know those little frozen microwave burritos? I used to eat them by the fistful. It wasn't until college that I started running, got Lasik. I bloomed pretty late. So I get you.

VUTHY. Wow, you my fuckin hero Glenn –

GLENN. Come live with us.

(short pause)

Ra told me about the deal with your mom's friend, and it's not right. It doesn't sit right with me.

VUTHY. So what.

GLENN. So come live with us.

VUTHY. She said you got no space –

GLENN. We'll make space. We'll get your stuff and…you might have to sleep on the futon for a while, but we'll get a bigger place. You'll get your own room.

You can transfer to Berkeley High or Oakland Tech. Whatever you want – take a look at both and decide for yourself.

(short pause)

VUTHY. No.

GLENN. Why not?

VUTHY. This is where I live. This is where I'm from. And I doan wanna go.

GLENN. Okay, but…think about it. Because –

I'm sorry about your mother.

And I know that I'm the last person in the world that you'd want to talk to about that, but I went through the same –

*(**VUTHY** goes into his room, slams the door.)*

Scene Two

(The apartment. Afternoon.)

(RA enters, looks around. The coast is clear.)

(She pulls HAN into the room, kisses him.)

(He takes a huge bite out of a burger.)

RA. You eat a lot.

(She sips out of an In-N-Out cup.)

HAN. I'm the biggest Cambodian in the world. Gots to ingest at least three thousand calories daily to maintain. You should see me at the temple on New Years, juss *eatin* – I scare myself.

RA. I didn't know you still went there.

HAN. Course I do. One of the monks taught me my hook shot.

RA. I was never into going there.

HAN. Yeah?

RA. I never learned the chants, I don't know what any of it means.

HAN. Hmmmm.

RA. When I'm there I feel like a tourist.

HAN. If you want, I could teach you.

RA. No. Thanks, but – I'm too far gone.

(beat)

So where'd you take Vuthy last night?

HAN. To a hooker.

RA. *(laughs)* No, for real: Where'd you take him?

HAN. The batting cages. I told him to say we was going to a movie 'cause some of my boys was gonna be there and I knew you wouldn't approve, so –

RA. Okay. Just tell me the truth from now on –

HAN. A'ight.

RA. And bring him back before ten.

HAN. Okay.

RA. Thanks for making him your sidekick.

HAN. Don't worry about it. I owe it to your ma –

RA. Stop saying that, will you? You don't owe anybody anything.

HAN. I was takin food out of your mouth.

RA. She always cooked more than she needed to. She loved seeing you eat. So did I. So it's a'ight.

HAN. *(smiling)* "A'ight," huh?

RA. *(grinning back at him)* Yes.

> *(beat)*

> She would've had a fit if she ever knew we were together.

HAN. Think so?

RA. She always pulled me away – by the ear – from guys like you. Hangin on the stoop, chain smokin, with your chains and your baggy clothes and your caps –

HAN. But she let me into your house.

RA. She knew you before you became one of those guys. When you were a skinny kid with a mop top and a big ol' adam's apple stickin out of your throat.

HAN. *(laughs)* That was a previous life.

RA. Yeah. You got all cool. I remember you waitin for me after school. Behind the chain link fence leaning on your shiny black car. You thought you were so cool lookin like that, all confident and dapper –

HAN. "Dapper"?

RA. Every Khmer boy wants to be a player. But you weren't like that. You knew that you didn't need to play.

> *(He puts his arm around her, holds her close.)*

HAN. So whatchu gonna do now?

RA. I don't know. What are you gonna do?

HAN. Don't know.

RA. You going to be good?

HAN. Yeah.

(She kisses him.)

RA. You're lying.

HAN. Maybe.

(He tries to kiss her.)

RA. Will you be good?

HAN. Will you stay?

RA. She wouldn't have wanted me to. Ma: I can picture the look of disappointment she'd throw me. For not becoming a doctor or not marrying a dentist from Agoura Hills –

HAN. You can still do that. The doctor part.

RA. Well, we'll see about that.

(beat)

After all you told me about her, a part of me is kind of – I don't know. Angry at her.

HAN. Why?

RA. For keeping all those things secret.

HAN. Your ma wanted to be what she was, *now,* in your eyes. Back in Cambodia, that was another life. You fly across the ocean and you leave it behind.

And she didn't tell you those things 'cause she thought she was protecting you –

RA. I don't want to be protected. Those things were a part of her. And I should've known so I could've talked to her about them.

(beat)

What hurts is realizing how little I know about my own mother.

(short pause)

You remember anything from when you were little? From when you were there.

HAN. What do you want me to tell you?

RA. Everything.

(HAN *lights a cigarette.*)

HAN. I was born in '76, my Ma, Pa, ran away from the Khmer Rouge in '79 –

RA. I already know the facts. But how did you feel?

HAN. *(Smiling slightly as he recollects this:)* Hungry. Felt hungry all the time. Insides-scooped-out hungry.

RA. Yeah?

HAN. Thirsty. Felt stiff. Sore from having to hold myself up. It's –

(He pauses, thinking.)

When the air's got a moist, humid sorta heat, it brings me back there. And that sticky, sweet smell of rotting things…garbage. Flies buzzing in little black clouds. Everything wet and dripping and falling apart.

(beat)

Some of my memories, they go so far back that I ain't sure if they're real. They're half dream, half real. And they're so long ago that I ain't sure what my mind made up –

RA. Yeah.

HAN. There's this…dream I keep havin.

RA. Yeah?

HAN. In it, it's… It's raining in big heavy drops. And I'm sitting alone in the mud –

RA. Where are you?

HAN. Don't know. I'm somewhere, lost…

(beat)

Then… I… My Ma and Pa find me.
And they pick me up.
And they carry me away…
But in my mind I know: They ain't mine.
And I'm thinkin… Maybe they mistook me for him, for their real son and –

RA. Han –

HAN. And they left him behind or didn't want to know he was dead, so –

RA. They took you.

HAN. Yeah – and I'm not sure if thass real or not –

RA. Your parents – you're their son. You look just like your Pa –

HAN. Maybe my mind made it all up. But it feels true. True in my bones, and…

You know what my Pa's like. My Ma was the same. Something back there broke them. Made em silent. They're like ghosts. So it makes me wonder if –

RA. You're the one they should've left behind.

HAN. Yeah –

RA. I know what you mean.

HAN. But Ra: You're the most together person I know.

RA. It looks that way, but… My bones feel different.

(beat)

Han – I think we should –

(HAN makes a move to go.)

HAN. I gotta go. There's something I gotta do –

RA. You gotta see a guy about a thing?

HAN. Can't make donuts forever.

RA. You're just like my Ma was. You're always rushing around –

HAN. I do what I got to –

RA. You're always onto the next thing and the next, always busy with your business –

(short pause)

Han –

HAN. Yeah.

RA. Do you promise to be good?

Scene Three

(The apartment.)

*(***GLENN*** works at his computer.)*

*(***VUTHY*** suddenly stomps in through the front door, tearful, agitated – he heads toward his room –)*

*(***RA*** bursts through the front door, goes after him –)*

RA. No you don't –

VUTHY. GET OFFA ME –

RA. You're gonna explain to me what you did –
     Why I'm getting calls from the Principal's office –

VUTHY. What do you care?

GLENN. Ra –

RA. Shut up.

(to **VUTHY***:)*

     You got two seconds before I smack you in the mouth.

VUTHY. So do it already –

(She smacks him the mouth –)

GLENN. Ra –

RA. You're gonna tell me what you were thinking –

VUTHY. Well you weren't there –

RA. WHAT THE FUCK WERE YOU THINKING.

VUTHY. YOU WEREN'T THERE. Those two Samoans was hen peckin me – I tried to ignore them. But one of em said "What are you gonna do now without your mama, mama's boy?" And I said doan say that, you say that again an you gonna regret it. And he says it again: "Whatchoo gonna do now without your mama?" And so I grabbed an extra sharp pencil and BAM MOTHERFUCKA! BAM! FUCK YOU, FUCK YOU! And I stabbed that shit through his cheek and into his teef –

RA. You coulda hit that kid in the eye –

VUTHY. Thass where I was aiming!

(She smacks him in the mouth again. He stands firm.)

GLENN. Ra, stop –

RA. This is just what I fuckin need right now –

VUTHY. Well I'm glad –

RA. JUST WHAT I FUCKIN NEED –

VUTHY. I'm goin to my room –

RA. They're talking expulsion –

VUTHY. Cool, expel me!

RA. That's what you want?

VUTHY. I can take the GED, be on my own –

RA. No, you can't –

VUTHY. How would you know, Ra? You hang out in Berkeley, drinkin green tea n' shit, you ain't here –

RA. I grew up here. And I made it through the same high school without stabbing anyone –

VUTHY. You're not the same as me. You was protected –

RA. No, I laid low and stayed out of trouble –

VUTHY. Well, I'm not you. I can't fuckin hide.

RA. You aren't even trying –

VUTHY. And fuck hiding anyway – I'm standing up. I'm gettin oppressed, and I'm standing up to my oppressors but you're on their side –

RA. What would Ma say right now? Do you know how –

VUTHY. What do you know about that –

RA. How ashamed she'd be –

VUTHY. Doan use Ma like that, or tell me how she'd feel, 'cause you doan know –

RA. She was my mother too –

VUTHY. How would you know when you weren't even here? You weren't at the hospital with her –

RA. Okay –

VUTHY. Sittin up there every night – worrying and wondering. So how tha fuck would you know? You just come back here and complain about having to close up her store and having to pack up her things and you don't give a fuck that she's gone –

(She tries to smack him again, but he catches her wrist –)

VUTHY. *(cont.)* An I'm still here, even if you wish that I was gone too.

RA. Don't say that.

VUTHY. But it's fuckin true. So lemme go to my room while it's still mine. And do what you always do: Run off, do whatever you want.

(He exits into his room, slams his door.)

(She stares at it, exasperated.)

GLENN. Ra –

RA. I'm sorry you had to see that.

GLENN. It's all right.

RA. You should go. It's been three days, you need to get back.

GLENN. It's okay. I can stay here as long as you need me –

RA. Glenn –

GLENN. Forget my attending, forget the studies –

RA. Things are a mess here – Vuthy –

GLENN. Then we'll take him with us.

(beat)

I've made a decision: I'm going to buy a place.

I talked to my uncle – he'll help me with the payments until I get my practice started. We'll get a two, three bedroom place in Oakland, maybe Piedmont –

RA. You don't have to –

GLENN. That way you can study instead of working so much. You can take AC Transit or BART to campus and you wouldn't have to pay for parking –

RA. Well, I don't –

GLENN. I'll help you pack everything up, we'll throw away what you don't need, start over fresh –

RA. Glenn: I'm not going back with you.

GLENN. What?

RA. This isn't working. This hasn't been working for –

GLENN. Where is this coming from?

RA. See, that's the problem – that you don't get it –

GLENN. Look: If I've been sleepwalking somehow –

RA. Hah –

GLENN. Tell me so that I know –

RA. You treat me like your pupil. Always one-upping me with your glorious anecdotes about Johns Hopkins, tellin me that if I grit my teeth, I'll make it –

GLENN. Okay –

RA. If I wanted to be patronized like this, I'd fuck my TA –

GLENN. Okay, so I'm an idiot and I don't know when to stop –

RA. And then you come down here trying to fix everything, making plans that I don't want to be a part of –

GLENN. I'm just trying to make things easier –

RA. Why? Because you've seen the shitty little apartment I grew up in –

GLENN. No –

RA. Because you feel sorry for me –

GLENN. That's not fair, Ra –

RA. I don't need my shit solved for me, Glenn –

GLENN. I'm just trying to help you –

RA. I don't want you to –

GLENN. Because I understand what's going on with your mother –

RA. No, you don't –

GLENN. Because I wanted to come down here for her funeral –

RA. Glenn –

GLENN. And you shut me down whenever I ask you anything about her –

RA. Because you can't –

GLENN. And now I'm waking up alone in the morning, wondering where you are –

RA. Glenn:

GLENN. Look – it doesn't matter.

Just don't put this on me, Ra.

Because I am trying. I am fucking trying –

RA. Glenn: You have no idea what losing her was like –

GLENN. When my dad passed away – stomach cancer – we were in hell but we dealt with it and moved on. And that's what you need to do – let it go, move on –

RA. Well, I don't know if this is what I want anymore. So you need to go, Glenn –

GLENN. No. Let's talk about this.

RA. What do you want me to say?

GLENN. I'm not just going to leave you behind.

RA. You wanna help me out?… Go. Go home.

Scene Four

(The apartment. Afternoon.)

(VUTHY draws on a sketchbook.)

(HAN watches him through the screen door, enters.)

HAN. Heard there's a Samoan kid who's gonna be drinking his food through a straw for the next few weeks.

VUTHY. *(distracted)* Yeah.

HAN. Hope he got a blender at home.

(short pause)

HAN. So how many days of suspension you got?

VUTHY. Two.

HAN. That ain't bad at all.

(Short pause. VUTHY puts down his pen.)

VUTHY. Han –

HAN. Yeah?

VUTHY. The last day of Ma's funeral, when we went to the place where she was cremated –

HAN. Uh-huh –

VUTHY. You know how you're supposed to walk towards the place where they cremate the body, and carry the candle an the incense and the flower?

HAN. Yeah –

VUTHY. And they tell you not to look back as you're walking in –

HAN. Uh-huh.

VUTHY. You're never supposed to look back... But I did.

HAN. Why?

VUTHY. I doan know.

(short pause)

VUTHY. I think... I wanted to see something.

HAN. You believe in ghosts, Vuthy?

VUTHY. I doan know. Do you?

HAN. I think… Sometimes people get lost, you know? They get lost on the way to their next life, and they wander, not knowin where to go to. But eventually, everyone gets reborn.

VUTHY. So you believe in bein reincarnated?

HAN. It's a good sorta thing to think about. Bein reborn. Clean.

VUTHY. But if you're reincarnated, you're a different person, right?

HAN. I think so.

VUTHY. I wanna be me forever, even after I die. I wanna remember everything I know.

(beat)

In Greek mythology, when you die they dip you into a river – makes you forget everything. Everything you are.

HAN. Mmmmm.

VUTHY. If they tried to dip me in there I would fuckin' run. Run from god, the devil, whatever. 'Cause I doan wanna forget. Doan wanna start at zero.

HAN. Well, you got a lot of good memories.

VUTHY. Naw. They ain't all good… But I still wanna keep 'em.

(short pause)

HAN. So you don't got school tomorrow?

VUTHY. No.

HAN. So I don't got to pick you up tomorrow?

VUTHY. You wouldn't be able to anyway.

HAN. Why's that.

VUTHY. 'Cause Donny Neak is gettin out tonight.

HAN. So?

VUTHY. So you gotta –

HAN. Yeah, I do.

VUTHY. You doan got to do what they say –

HAN. I got to. Thass the core of what we are, of how we tied together –

VUTHY. But you're a good guy.

(short pause)

HAN. When the Khmer Rouge ruled, good people died first. People who shared what they had, sacrificed themselves. The Khmer people that died first were the good ones. Same as it ever was. Good people don't survive –

VUTHY. My Ma survived.

HAN. Your Ma wasn't always good.

(beat)

And don't think that I'm a good guy, Vuthy, 'cause I don't wanna be one. So stop fuckin askin me to do that.

(**HAN** starts to head out –)

VUTHY. Donny's gonna be waitin for you. Him an his brothers – they're waitin –

HAN. I know.

VUTHY. But you gotta do what you're supposed to –

HAN. Because I owe people, Vuthy.

VUTHY. And we doan matter.

HAN. Thass not what I'm sayin.

VUTHY. You say you're my *bong proh* but I doan fuckin believe it – you put Donny up there an' say you and he was twins but then you turn around on him just because someone else told you to –

HAN. Vuthy –

VUTHY. But you have to. 'Cause you owe people.

But what about me?

HAN. Listen:

VUTHY. You're gonna be gone and leave me alone again –

Or I'm gonna watch them burn your body too –

HAN. If I could change things, I would –

VUTHY. But you can't.

'Cause if you're waitin for your next life to come, you doan have to give a fuck about this one.

Scene Five

(Night. The front steps of a Buddhist temple.)

(RA sits there, watches the traffic go by.)

(HAN enters, sees her.)

HAN. Ra –

RA. Han.

RA. *(looking up at the building –)* The temple.

HAN. You asked me for a place to meet.

How long's it been since we've been here together?

RA. I don't know.

HAN. A lot of New Years have gone by.

Loved seeing your ma here on New Years: Big smile on her face. Red dress, orange scarf.

I made a choice: Thass how I'm gonna remember her.

(short pause)

I'm movin out of my Pa's place. Eddie Diep's got a spare room, and…I think it's about time I got out on my own.

(beat)

I'ma be there starting on Tuesday. You're gonna come by, right?

RA. Han –

(She's troubled; he tries to put his arms around her –)

HAN. What's the matter?…Is everything –

RA. I called you because I didn't want to talk to you about this in front of Vuthy.

HAN. What's wrong?

RA. I know about Donny Neak.

(short pause)

HAN. Ra: It's going to be fine. Everything's –

RA. What are you going to do.

HAN. What I have to.

RA. You have a choice –

HAN. Listen:

RA. Tell them to fuck off and leave Donny alone –
   His family – they're just gonna stand by and let that go?

HAN. I got no choice.

RA. What happens when they find you? …You know what they'll do to you –

HAN. We got a place I can go to up in Sac, lay low for a while –

RA. I left him for you: Glenn.

HAN. Ra –

RA. I will stay here with you if you get out of this –

HAN. I can't.

RA. I will stay here for you if you stay here with me –

HAN. Give me some time. Let me do what I got to, and I'll come back for you.

   (short pause)

RA. And after that, what's it gonna be like? You and me.

HAN. It'll be like it was before –

RA. I'm gonna be lying awake, wondering where you are, waiting by my bedroom window hoping to hear your car in the driveway…

HAN. No. I'ma take care of you –

RA. With envelopes fulla twenties that came from junkies, from breaking into peoples' houses –

HAN. Thass not what I'm sayin –

RA. You gonna bring Vuthy into your shit, too?

HAN. I'd never do that, Ra.

   (beat)

   Look: After this I'll get out.

RA. You're telling me this shit like you've never told it to me before.

HAN. After this we'll leave. You, me, Vuthy. We'll go somewhere –

RA. Where would that be?

HAN. I'll find a way.

RA. I can't, Han. I'm not –

I won't go back to that.

HAN. Ra –

RA. No. I've come too far.

(short pause)

HAN. I was always jealous of you, you know that?

RA. Why.

HAN. You had a family. Your ma.

RA. Well, what would she say if she knew what you're gonna do?

HAN. Ra: I was just a kid that grew up next to you. I helped her in her store, she fed me when she could, but that was it.

(RA pauses, thinking.)

RA. When I left for Berkeley, gettin in my crappy car to go, you know how she was looking at me?... Worried. Hopeful. And from the way she was lookin at me, I knew: She'd be thinking about me till I came back home.

HAN. Why you tellin me this, Ra?

RA. Because the last time you left her, did you look back at my ma as you were walking away?

Because I was there.

And you should've seen how she was lookin at you.

(beat)

You know what she'd tell you to do, right?

HAN. What.

RA. Run.

(He considers this, staring into her eyes.)

(He kisses her. She relaxes into it.)

(But they let each other go.)

Who am I gonna talk to about her? About Ma?

HAN. You still got a family.
Someone to talk to.
So talk to him.

(And she watches him as he goes.)

Scene Six

(The apartment. Late at night.)

(VUTHY sits at the kitchen table staring at the skull.)

VUTHY. There's this story that my Ma used to tell me. About this great king who left his country, his peoples, because he wanted to learn how to do magic. So that when there was a drought he could be a rainmaker. And when there was a famine he could make crops rise outta the fields. And so he traveled to a distant kingdom where there was this great wizard, this teacher. And the wizard taught him how to make rain fall outta the sky, and fruit fall outta the trees. And the wizard taught the king how to transform into all sortsa animals, real and mythical.

And when he had learned everything he could learn, the king started his journey back to his people. But he got lost in a strange land, in a foreign country he had never seen before.

He wandered for days. He began to starve, wondered if he'd ever see his home, his peoples again. But then he had an idea: He would use his magic to turn into a tiger and catch something to eat.

So he spoke the right spell and his body transformed – fangs, claws like razors. And he felt more powerful, more majestic than he had ever felt as a king.

And he was easily able to catch a stag, and he tore into it with his teeth –

And it was an easy thing to catch the next one, and the next one. And he loved life as a tiger – he began to forget that he was ever human – that he was ever a king.

And those memories, of his people and his country, turned into a distant dream. This had always been his life. And sometimes he would sleep and dream of being a man. But when he woke up, he knew that he had always been a tiger. And he always would be.

(beat)

VUTHY. *(cont.)* That's what my Ma said.
But what I wanna know is if…
You think that…
Tigers can change.

Scene Seven

(The apartment. Morning.)

(RA knocks on VUTHY's door. He answers.)

RA. I'm doing laundry later, so if you need anything washed let me know.

(VUTHY remains silent.)

I'm out of underwear. Gonna have to start wearing stuff twice –

VUTHY. Ew.

(VUTHY lopes into the kitchen, pours himself a bowl of imitation Froot Loops.)

RA. Hey – when you're ready to go I'll take you to school.

VUTHY. You don't have to.

RA. It's fine.

VUTHY. 'Cause you should know that those Samoans is out there lookin to murder me.

RA. Well, then they'll have to murder me too.

VUTHY. They might actually do that.

RA. Oh, by the way, there's something I wanted to ask you about –

(She opens up the cookie jar, takes out the skull.)

RA. Whose skull is this?

VUTHY. It's mine.

RA. Uh-huh. Where'd you get it?

VUTHY. Ebay. It's a museum quality replica, thirty-nine dollars shipped.

RA. Why you spendin money on stuff like this?

VUTHY. I doan know. I like having it around.

(beat)

It reminds me of Choeung Ek. Seeing all those skulls on the rack.

RA. Why you want to think about that?

VUTHY. 'Cause it makes me think of Ma. Makes me think about whether I was worth it.

RA. Worth what, Vuthy?

VUTHY. Worth everything she did. Everything she had to do to make it over here.

RA. You can't think about that all the time, Vuthy.

VUTHY. Why not.

RA. I don't know. Spend some time being happy.

VUTHY. That's why I think about it. It reminds me to try... Being happy.

(beat)

I saw Om Sang last night.

Did you hear about Han?

RA. No. What happened.

VUTHY. He's gone.

He left in the middle of the night, and Om Sang don't know where he went.

Nobody knows.

RA. Huh...well. Good for him.

VUTHY. He left without sayin anything, Ra.

RA. Well, I'm sure he's thinking about you.

(short pause)

Get your stuff. We gotta go –

(There's a knock at the front door.)

(GLENN enters. He is a disheveled shell of himself.)

GLENN. Hi.

RA. Hi.

GLENN. I was going to leave today, drive back up... But I needed to come by here first –

RA. Glenn –

GLENN. I know. But I've gotta ask you: Do you think I'm incapable of understanding you?

RA. It's not just that.

GLENN. But that's the biggest thing, right?

RA. Yeah.

GLENN. All right. So I've been thinking about it a lot and I've figured it out: Yes. I am incapable of ever truly understanding you.

RA. Okay.

GLENN. But I want to. And it's the same thing as – let me get this right –

(He pulls out a piece of paper, reads:)

"Wanting to play center for the Lakers. And I'll never be able to, but that doesn't negate the fact that I still really, really want to" – what the fuck..?

RA. *(smiling)* Uh-huh.

GLENN. It doesn't matter what happened in the past between us. We can fix it. And –

RA. You want something to drink?

GLENN. No. I just – I want you to hear what I'm saying –

RA. I do. I hear you.

GLENN. And if you still want me to go, I will. I'll go, but I want you to hear me out.

RA. I have.

GLENN. Okay. So... Should I go?

RA. Well –

GLENN. WAIT –

(He fumbles through his pockets, takes something out –)

(It's an object just like one of Ma's objects.)

I found it in this little store on Anaheim street. I saw it in the window, and remembered you have a whole lot of them here, so... Here.

(He offers it to **RA.** *)*

I thought you might want one more to add to the collection.

RA. Glenn, you should know that these aren't mine.

GLENN. *(to* **VUTHY***:)* And I don't suppose they're yours –

VUTHY. Nope.

(GLENN carefully examines Ma's objects.)

GLENN. Her family – did any of them –

RA. No.

They killed her brother and her sisters, one by one.
She dug their graves.

GLENN. But she survived.

RA. Yeah.

She ran away.

(beat)

Those things that happened back there: You wouldn't know it just by looking at her.

When she'd laugh, she'd squeeze her eyes shut, laugh with her whole body.

She used to sing little pieces of songs –

But that was her way: To just keep on going –

VUTHY. Ra –

RA. You ready?

GLENN. Do you need a ride to school?

(RA looks at VUTHY, then –)

RA. We'll see.

GLENN. 'Cause I –

RA. I'll call you. Okay?

(He looks at her, understands.)

GLENN. Okay.

(GLENN smiles, exits.)

RA. Hey: I gotta tell you something.

VUTHY. What.

RA. This afternoon you'd better start putting your stuff in boxes and start loading them in my car.

And you better let me know what kind of snacks you want for the trip, because it's a long drive up to Berkeley –

VUTHY. What?

RA. It's a six, seven hour drive up to Berkeley, and we aren't stopping for McDonalds –

VUTHY. Please doan fuck with me, Ra.

RA. – And in the mornings, you'd better put the futon away like you said you would –

VUTHY. For real? –

RA. – You need to go through your stuff and give away whatever you don't want. I don't wanna have to lug all your junk up there –

(He hugs her.)

RA. But do me a favor –

VUTHY. What.

RA. Don't worry me so much. I'm not like Ma. I can't take it.

VUTHY. A'ight.

RA. And you've gotta help me pack.

(Re: Ma's objects –)

We've got a lot of things to wrap up.

VUTHY. Okay.

RA. I'm gonna get started. We gotta go.

(She goes into her mother's bedroom.)

*(**VUTHY** sees the skull, picks it up, speaks to it:)*

VUTHY. I don't think I need to ask you for much anymore.
But doan worry: I'ma take you with me.
And if you see my Ma, tell her that it's a'ight for her to go on to whatever place she's got to go to next.
And tell her I'm sorry for leaving Long Beach behind.
'Cause this place was more than good to her, you know?
She was born back there, in the same place you were.
But this…
This is where she lived.

End of Act Two

End of Play

ABOUT THE PLAYWRIGHT

Michael Golamco is an LA-based playwright and screen-writer. The New York premiere of his play *Year Zero* opened at Second Stage in May 2010. It previously received an acclaimed run at the Victory Gardens Theatre in Chicago and was the Grand Prize Winner of Chicago Dramatists' Many Voices Project. His play *Cowboy Versus Samurai* has had several productions since its premiere in NYC, including in Canada and Hong Kong. Michael is the recipient of the 2009 Helen Merrill Award and is a member of New Dramatists. He is currently working on new play commissions for South Coast Repertory and Second Stage Theatre.

As a screenwriter, Michael's film *Please Stand By* was presented at the 2009 Tribeca Film Festival's On Track film development program. His short film, *Dragon of Love*, was awarded Best Short Film at the Hawaii International Film Festival and ran in regular rotation on the Sundance Channel.